SHAWN and KEEPER

and the Birthday Party

Happy Birthday SHAWN

by Jonathan London

illustrated by Renée Williams-Andriani

PUFFIN BOOKS

For Sean and Keeper, and Skeena too—J.L.
For Maggie, Ellen, and Joseph—R.W.-A.

PUFFIN BOOKS
Published by the Penguin Group
Penguin Putnam Books for Young Readers, 345 Hudson Street, New York, New York 10014, U.S.A.
Penguin Books Ltd, 27 Wrights Lane, London W8 5TZ, England
Penguin Books Australia Ltd, Ringwood, Victoria, Australia
Penguin Books Canada Ltd, 10 Alcorn Avenue, Toronto, Ontario, Canada M4V 3B2
Penguin Books (N.Z.) Ltd, 182-190 Wairau Road, Auckland 10, New Zealand

Penguin Books Ltd, Registered Offices: Harmondsworth, Middlesex, England

First published by Dutton Children's Books and Puffin Books,
members of Penguin Putnam Books for Young Readers, 1999

3 5 7 9 10 8 6 4 2

Text copyright © Jonathan London, 1999
Illustrations copyright © Renée Williams-Andriani, 1999
All rights reserved

Cataloging-in-Publication data is available upon request from the Library of Congress.

Puffin Books ISBN 0-14-130407-3

Puffin® and Easy-to-Read® are registered trademarks of Penguin Books USA Inc.

Printed in Hong Kong
Set in ITC Century Book

Reading Level 1.6

...eeper

...the same day.

They grew up together.

When Shawn was a baby,

Keeper was a puppy.

When Shawn turned one,

Keeper turned one too.

Now Shawn was going to be six.

And so was Keeper.

Tomorrow was the big day!

Keeper helped Shawn choose a cake.

"Strawberry!" Shawn told Mom.

"Woof!" barked Keeper.

Keeper helped Shawn

pick a piñata for the party.

"A pig or a dog?" asked Shawn.

"Woof!" barked Keeper.

"A dog it is," said Shawn.

Keeper helped Shawn
blow up balloons.
"Pop!" went every balloon
that Keeper tried to catch.

That night, Shawn lay awake.

He was thinking about the party.

Keeper lay awake beside him.

"Oh boy," said Shawn. "I can't wait!"

When Shawn woke up,

he smelled the cake baking.

"Yum!" said Shawn,

and they ran downstairs.

"Can I have a bite?" asked Shawn.

"No cake now!" said Mom.

"Help Dad hang the balloons."

"Can I have a bite?" asked Shawn.

"No cake now!" said Dad.

"Help me hang the piñata."

"Can I have a bite?" asked Shawn.

"No cake now!" said Mom.

"Your friends are here."

And the party began!

Shawn and his friends did the limbo.

So did Keeper.

They played pin the tail on the donkey.

Keeper played too.

Shawn and his friends

hit the piñata.

Keeper ran and hid.

They had hot dogs, chips, and drinks.

Then Shawn yelled, "The cake! The cake!

It's time for the cake!"

"Oh no!" Mom shouted.

"The cake is gone!"

She held up an empty cake pan.

"Keeper!" shouted Shawn.

Shawn and his friends went hunting
for Keeper and the cake.
They looked in the kitchen.

Shawn and his friends went hunting

for Keeper and the cake.

They looked in the kitchen.

She held up an empty cake pan.

"Keeper!" shouted Shawn.

They looked in the bathroom.

They looked in the yard.

"Keeper!" shouted Shawn.

Keeper came over.

He looked sheepish.

"Where's my cake?" asked Shawn.

"Here it is!" said Dad.

"Surprise!"

He had added Keeper's name to the cake.

"Hurray!" everybody shouted.

Shawn gave Keeper a hug.

Together, Shawn and Keeper

blew out the candles.

"Did you make a wish, Keeper?"

asked Shawn.

"Woof!" barked Keeper.

Keeper got his wish.

He got a chunk of cake.

"Happy birthday!" sang Shawn.

"Woof!" barked Keeper.

And when they tore open their presents,
they howled with joy.

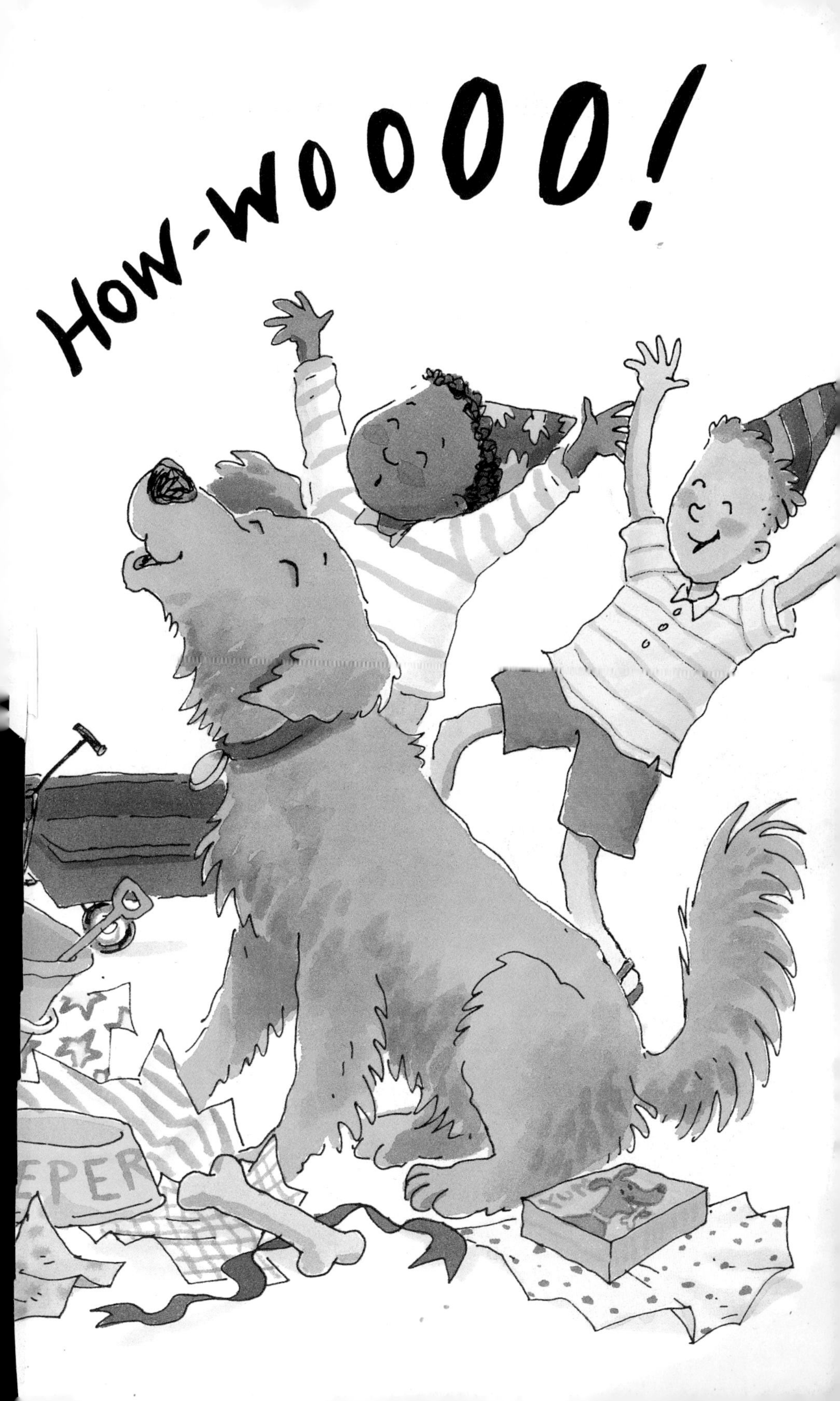
How-woooOO!